WHEN HORSES FLY

THE KARANKAWA OF TERLINGUA

∽

AN ADULT CHRISTIAN NOVELLA

BY

F. H. GRISSINO

-With Afterword and Sermon-

The Karankawa of Terlingua™

**ADULT THEMES
NOT SUITABLE FOR CHILDREN**

Genre: Christian/Native American/Spiritual Fiction

This book is not intended to be an exhaustive discourse on history or doctrine.

ISBN: 0615614221
ISBN-13: 9780615614229

TO THE BLESSINGS OF DISCOVERY

- And of its mysterious ways -

∽

Introduction:
Man's Gift To God

I feel strongly that the many religions and doctrines existing today were created to help man understand the mysteries of life that are dumped at his front door........ and to come to grips with those ordeals that confront him at his back porch......

-But were these codes we now live by just mysteriously appeared and impressed upon our ancestors, magically arriving through obscured clouds as thunder ?

No, they were not merely found nor simply given to us - they found their way to us as only we could hear the echo, as only we could discover the resonance of our being, as only we could unearth the many intonations for ourselves.

-But many of us would say that our beliefs were inspired and endowed to us through the Graces of God; however, we forget that those particular graces which we allegedly practice today remain as those that we chose to adopt in our pursuit towards evolving within God's Kingdom. No matter what scripture has been written, it is what we adopt into our hearts through the test of time and experience that creates it as everlasting.

In our search through clouds to wind exposed
        In our journey to emerge with earth unopened
            We invisibly acquire but not perceive
The inequities of legacy
                with its favours of apparition
    With its souvenirs of discovery
                exposed as thunder unearthed
                Disguised as the true gift of man
                    to God
                As the Gift of reciprocity

Our Long Prologue of Native Beginnings

- In the beginning we are born in the image of God - but do we know who we really are? ....We are the creation of God - but do we know where we really came from?

- Alongside the moving migration of everlasting life and passing time - do we really know who are ancestors were after all?

- For although the Lord gives us eternal life, we presently have one life to live.........For although God guides us, he cannot, and he will not, make our future decisions for us..........

We see that our Bible does more than chronicle the evolution of our being, our development of faith, our concept and acknowledgement of sin; we see of the many Proverbs and Gospels, collectively distilling the laws of a budding and sophisticated Christian civilization in progress - and we see that this also was collectively bothe the efforts of God AND Man - that which has collectively evolved into every man's birthright, much as Jesus has been acknowledged to be both of God AND Man....

Insightful yet deliberate - spontaneous yet flexible - I feel that it is these quint-essential combinations that mark the miracle within Man's evolution of de-velopment; the essence in which we can withness HIM; for a man might unquestionably accept the words of faith from a precipice of purile innocence - but he is also enabled to understand a lifetime of truth as he looks from his cliff of experience.

We now see that this dimension of man's development - the merging of spirit and instinct - eternally marks THE BEGINNING; and within this sense, any polarization we might feel between the LAWS of creationism and the CON-CEPTS of evolutionism should be set aside for us to emerge toward one con-cept encompassing faith in working reciprocity.

Of giving and receiving
within the unlimited potential
of growing confines
Begets all acts God and Man
As the moon depends on the sun
As the sunrise of war
depends on the hopeful sunset
in peace

.......And it shall be within this story that when we ask the seemingly simple questions of our origin, we will receive no precise answers from God, with those many innocent questions becoming turbulently complicated amidst the uncertain events of life.

As man instinctively utilizes much of his faith to achieve a synchronicity between his being and his world, he finds that much polarization is necessarily set aside. His instinct is to find that one, united answer existing among the many separate ones. Suddenly, it will not be as simple as science versus the wills of God. Because for lack of a better argument, science cannot. And out of plain principle, God will not.

You see, God wants us to DISCOVER - that is much of his plan. Without this simple concept, there is no realization of his prescence to begin with................

- And within the confines of this story we will ask another question -

When one discovers the truth about their origins, either intentionally or accidentally, does the merit of that knowledge alter our own perspective- our own balance- own personal relationship with life and those around us ?   Yes it does - and we could merely call it "The Irony of God's Will"....

......For it is not only the creation of our presence, but the understanding of its evidence that summons the desire of our life. It is a presence marking evidence to all beginnings. It is a presence that will ask us in moments of agony, "Then who might I- could I- have been ?"

4

The balance of our presence
    As knowledge invisible
For seeing that
    Because
Not withstanding
    We are
So invisibly so
    As We will
            Be seen

It is when we discover reciprocally that our presence IS evidence of our native beginnings, it is then that we discover that God needs us as much as we need him; It then becomes evident that as we approach our origins, we cannot capriciously choose or pick this one essential aspect of our lives; with this now known, we can pose another question:

- We have a Spirit inside of us - do we really UNDERSTAND who it is ?

Is it HIS breath ?
    Breaths of one or many
Of those before and after
    among us
Of who have lived just once
    or once never died
Of those walking the skies
    wandering a Universe
            That knows no path
                Until it touches one of us ?

WHEN HORSES FLY
THE KARANKAWA OF TERLINGUA

war bunny

Now many suppose I am fairly old now, considerably 8 years in dog years, of which now I can now fondly reminisce about my redundant experience with human socialization; this happened to be my very first visit to the Town Dentist at 12 years old, my teeth orange in color for which I was very proud ; for I had attained formidable neighborhood status as The Great Cannibal Pumpkin of All Hollows Eve.

"You haven't been eating mice, have you ?" the old dentist inferred timidly.

"No Sir, just lizards-just the tails." I fancied the creation in quick response to his illusionary question. Little did I know what he already DID know just by being a dentist in the small town of Chinnyswitch.....

He then appeared suddenly mortified - and puzzled at the same time.
"I don't hear the word 'Sir' very often, my honey-bun....where did you learn to say that ?"

"When Tarzan talks to the English Prince.........A Prince from England tried to kill Tarzan and steal his jungle, but his friend, The Lion of the Plains, killed and ate the prince......and Tarzan had warned him he would give 'im respect, but he wad'nt goin' ta' be no Prince while messin' aroun' in his jungle........."

I was earlier warned too late by Dr. Diction. "Ho, Bunny, I suppose IT served him right - AND the correct grammar to use is 'wasn't' !......So . Now, THAT, my little Bunny, is called WAR,'" as the dentist whinced through his magnifying monacle. "SO what DOES our little Bunny know about WAR ?"

Both he and my mother nervously laughed by my side. They both were worried I would lose all of my orange teeth that day - but I knew inside my Heart that they were stuck up in there just fine.

"............WELL, Tarzan says that there is no such thing as war when every-one knows where they belong, what is theirs, and that they must eat what they kill." I thought this sounded rather paintly civilized, my wild canvass lending its blank expression to cultured innocence.....

The Dentist's response was hesitated with punctuation. "Well, NOW, I SUP-POSE Tarzan is right, Bunny - I would dare hate to savour the taste of my Mother in Law - not at least until she brought the Packard back HOPEFULLY in one piece !!!"..........

"-SO, I suppose we all covet that which we cannot have, you KNOW, Bunny?" as his eyes slipped onto my mother's large chest, pinned innocently with a big Rose I had picked for her that morning.
".......-AND DOES Tarzan's Golden Rule ALSO apply to Mrs. Higgins PRIZED Rose Bushes, my War-Bunny ?"

My mother almost fainted, either from anxiety or embarrassment, that we shall never know - as the Dentist laid his monacle down for prognosis..........

A microbial miracle it 'twas; for it was nothing The Dentist had ever seen in his lifetime ; the orange plaques had formed a protective barrier , preventing any bacterial decay.

"No more mice tails for you, little lady," he peering at me in amazement, as though he would never see me again.........

"And easy on Mrs. Higgins roses and tomatoes, for they are actually full of sugars, good sugars nontheless."

.....There was no fooling a seasoned dentist who had seen just about every-thing in everyone's life wedged in-between their teeth ......

Scandalous conceptions knead
        Into man's civilized kingdoms
To bear its dread of silence
        That breed his lineage of secrets
The unknown but a haunting
        to one's lonely soul
                but one that you know very well

10

As the spirit of a young girl
　　　who knows they want her love
　　　and need her respect and trust
　　　　　But never give it to them
　　She demands
　　　　　as she steals the candy
　　　　　　　from your hand
　　　　　　　　and runs away with your laughter
　　Silently revealing
　　　　　That you will never earn
　　　　　　　The lineage of her secrets

∽

James 4-2: "From whence come wars and fightings among you ? Ye lust and have not; Ye kill and desire to have, and cannot obtain; Ye fight and war, yet ye have not, because ye ask not."

the universe

The Town Veterinarian told us that "a dog always knows where he wants to be, and where he wants to go" - as in reference to relieving himself, I had supposed………

-And So It Is Upon weaning knee and elbow out the back door, I spent all of my childhood in the back yard. This wonderful yard, replete with a Beagle puppy and three huge doghouses to house us during the cold Lunar nights, to protect us during the hot days of Mars' intense fury.

For I had so willed myself that our wretched house would never, ever heave its noises upon me at night, whispering at me with its mysterious retributions of the past; for now, I know as I suspected then, that my ancestors never lived in permanent houses as we know of them today.

-And I secretly understood this not as written or spoken words, but through invisible symbols seen in my dreams; instincts unheard, feelings unspoken; an invisible knowledge that The Great Unknown Universe must be earned with one's fear before receiving its trust.

෩

John 4-18: "There is no fear in love; but perfect love casteth out fear; because fear hath torment. He that feareth is not made perfect in love."

For it becomes
        Realized
                Our first discovery into Fear
                        Will ask of us many questions
Was it born
        or was it made
Is it as it is
        or is it the sense
                Of what will be
Does it happen
        In a fleeting instant
                Or does it grow
                        Slowly in time ?
As dense stars crowding
                lush skies at night
        Do Willow grasses
                Breeze past
                        Star grasses sparse ?
When cool breezes answer
        Then comfort
                Flies across
        Stirring blades of young light
                To soon bring with it
                        its dark question grown old
For a new universe
                Has suddenly been born
Who Knows no fear
        But for breath belonging
                within a new verse
                        from another universe
                                Realized now
                                        Inside of a place
                                                within a moment's time

epicurean explorations

Mesquite beans
    In the pocket of my jeans
Honey from flowers
    Baths from water towers
Free Bees
    And plucked fruit trees
The miracle of Lizard tails
    By Abundance hails
      As fecundity goes
        like Mrs. Higgins Roses and Tomatoes...........

But by the age of six, the Laws of Genetics and the Laws of Civilization were not agreeing with one or the other, being that none agreed with another, or nothing agreed with the other.

The Bathtub and The Toilet expressed frightful dangers for me. Straddling the line between poetry and parody was my father, who referred to the latter as 'The King's Throne, imported from Rome'.

This vacuum of violent, rushing water - that appeared suddenly in a violent flood - then disappearing again - its unknown depths desiring to suck me into its bottomless pit deep inside the earth.

So my father hosed off muddy Beagle and I every very weekend with his added splashes to the barbecue. Beagle and I always went outside to bathroom, in the corners of the soft, loamy yard, I myself felt it was safer and more sanitary than falling down into the hole of a commode.

This 'hestitation' to toilet train became my dad's stalwart criteria to gain my admission to see the town psychologist, The Great 'Doc' Bannon......

My friend Thom

Thomas was the son of The Great Dr. Bannon. He was considered the smart-est kid in town; for in the night he read every word his father precisely wrote on just about everyone in town.

I would jump out of the bushes and wrestle out his every word on his way back from Sunday school, this Little Man just brimming with knowledge and male confidence.

"Barley ran the Roman Army, and Jesus was kidnapped to make more, and when he wouldn't make any, they nailed him to a cross......My Dad says you would be good girl for me to marry, but you would have to go to Sunday school with me and read about how the World was made."

"Sounds good, Thom," I replied. "I would like someone to cook and to read stories to me."

"No, Francy, you do not get it," he angrily blustered. " It is not just a story. It is the truth. Eve has to do all the cooking. My Dad said that you have 'Penis Envy'. I think he is right."

Before I could ask what that was, his pants went to his knees. So I got real close and inspected whatever it was that had got my attention.

"I have a magnifying glass in my pocket if you want it," Thom snorted snottily. So I looked real hard through the glass, and it was not such a big thing after all. Not in the way Thom was parading it about, any way. It looked merely like a little pink caterpillar before it turns into a butterfly and flies away..........

............-And I was not sure exactly what I had discovered............

But
　　Just that
　　　　No more than
　　　　　　Perfectly
　　　　　　　Nevertheless
　　　　　　　　No less than
　　　　　　　　　merely nontheless

"That's no big deal !" I snorted back. "I can grow one of those. My Grandfather says that Vick's ointment can grow hair on an Indian's chest. He should know. He is an Indian and he showed me the two hairs on his chest. I'm gonna go home 'n put some Vick's on mine down there and grow a cat-pillar longer and fatter than that."

Thom's eyes got real big like a pie was to pop out of his mother's oven.

I actually did think that I should be able to grow one of those; my Grandpa always told me that you had inside of you everything you needed to do anything you needed to do and to become anything you needed to be. As an Indian, this was his belief that life was adaptation.

You not only were constantly changing day by day, but you were able to elicit anything you needed from within yourself. This was survival.

Everything that had ever existed upon this earth was inside of you waiting to come out and express itself; you just asked God for the ability to command and control what you wanted when you wanted it.
　　　　　………….This was faith………….

∽

Genesis 3-1: "And He said, Who told thee that thou wast naked ? Hast thou eaten of the tree, whereof I com-manded thee that thou shouldest not eat ?"

20

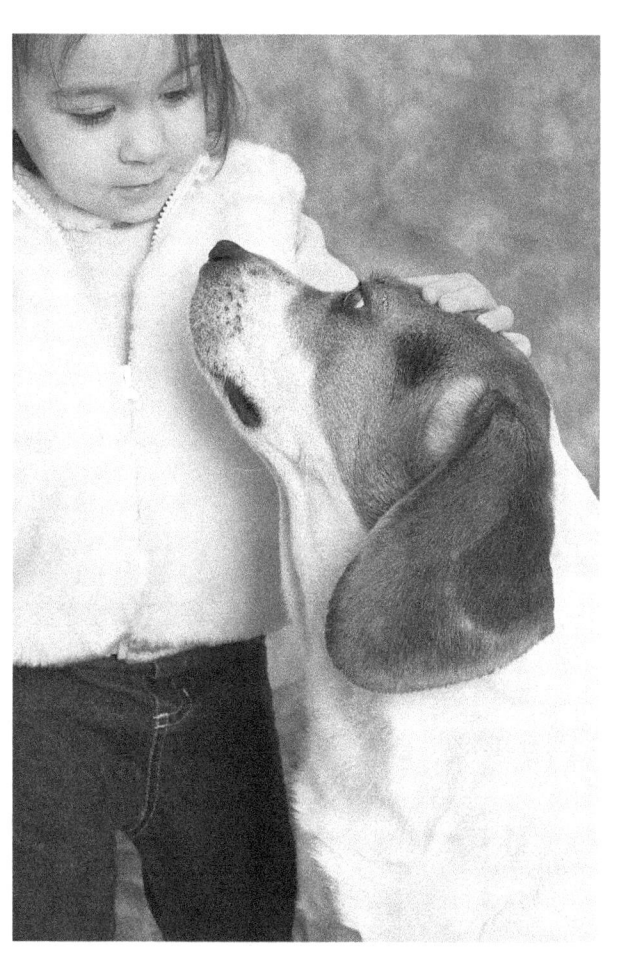

eggs, bacon and darla bannon

Twice a week, Beagle & I rushed into the living room for bacon & eggs and to watch 'Tarzan' on the TV; for these celebrated late afternoons would teach us what to drink, what to smoke, and what hairspray to use; and what we may wish to eat with our favorite chef, Julia Child.....

Those loud commercials became comforting resonance within the mute dissonance of the living room, a silence sighing imminent drones from the refrigerator .

Dressed in white garb, the refrigerator had become another evil device to fear. It resembled the town doctor as it ferociously 'walked' toward us when the motor came on. Within our Known Universe it was the doctor who decided who lived and who died, who would suffer in silence; the refrigerator decided who would eat and who would starve.

But not for me, for I had discovered independence through contempt, In much the same way when one discerns and decides to be either a boy or a girl. My little roaming Beagle had taught me that if fear was the biggest motivator, then need, greed and charm were going to be your companion to getting something when you wanted it .

And you better be versed in where to go and when to get it. This dilemma of fickle nature led me into the discovery of flattery, or as Grandpa called it "A little Hokum - that stuff that comes out of your mouth and other places on your body"..............

..........And it seemed that everyone in town had discovered the Beautiful Mizz Darla, Doctor Bannon's vivacious wife, who they all said smelled like money; so Beagle and I followed Thom home one day to see just what that smelled like and to make pests of ourselves.........

23

It was the scent
    Of Honeysuckle and hairspray
Her hair glistening like
    A big sugared mound
       Of cotton candy
          It was her way
Her red shoes painted
      Upon her feet
        Like lipstick dandy

"So how is your momma, Francy ?" Darla puckered as I confidently approached the back door For I lived on the other side of the railroad tracks, and my mother did Darla's ironing. Beagle sniffed with approval.

"Ma'am, she got some hairspray fro' the TV, but she doesn't know how to use it, and so she just sprays it around the house." Yes, flattery involves asking for advice. Beagle moved forward with a wagging tail.

We were almost in the house when Darla stopped us at the back porch.
"Oh Francy, get 'yer momma over here and I'll show her how to use that stuff. You can even spray the dinner with it and it will look good for hours if the man is late."

Beagle wrinkled up his nose in a whimper. Reject advice about food. She does not know we are budding prepubescent gourmets.

"-And is that your Daddy, the one over at the car dealership with the big muscles ? He looks just like Hercules, he does, with that beard and those ho-ho's so big and strong......."
Mizz Darla's lips puckered even bigger, like a lizard slurping a fly a river's bank away.

"Yes ma'am, he my Daddy all right, he can lift an engine with one hand and he can put some torque inside your motor." This sealed the golden opportunity to get those free pancakes that Thom had promised me on our way over.

Beagle jumped on my leg. We were certain we would soon be in the house. Soon.

But not so fast. Darla still had her toe and heel wedged like an ice pick in the door jamb, keeping us confined to the porch.

"Oh, Francy," Darla swooned, "I'm sure he CAN...........Now you tell your Daddy when you get home that Mizz Darla is coming in to get her oil changed - 'cause next week we are all going with the Doctor to San Antonio in the new Caddy ! Now I just know you and Thom will love the trip !"

"Mom, Francy wants her pancakes NOW !" Thom torted in boredom.

The porch was cooled with hanging Geraniums and wicker. I would not have wanted to be anywhere else - not even in Darla's gilded house replete with a Bidet Fountain........Imagine ! - a toilet that was a fountain ! Thom said it always felt good after a butt whipping..........

I had learned a humble lesson well. Men can beg almost as good as dogs do ; they just expect too much too soon ; and patience will be the foundation of all things to wait for.......

∽

Matthew 7-8 : 'For every one that asketh receiveth; and he that seeketh findeth; and to him that knocketh it shall be opened'............'Or what man is there of you, whom if his some ask bread, will he give him a stone ?'

'Grandpa comes to town'

It comes our beginning of Spring
        When the warmth emotion of nighttime sun
                Has met its enduring end
And the song of cool morning air
              Brings the Spirit of Mist
                    To be born yet again

"Your carburetor is smokin' bad, Old Man !" my Dad hollered to Grandpa as he chugged into the driveway. "Stop, old man, let me get the waterhose on it !"

And out of the misty smoke and Holy fire, came MY Grandpa, just to see ME. But his attention was towards the house next door..

Grandpa turned and hollered into the window next to our driveway. "I'll get Mary Higgins next door to fix it - she has hands like a grease monkey - I should know - we dated - REMEMBER, MARY ?" He was in good form and had brought lots of 'stuff,' what my Mother called 'unwrapped presents'. And lots of Beer. My favorite food.

Good bubbles in your nose
        Your face glows
                Talking in prose
                        that no one knows

"You dirty old Injun, you rabbit killer," screamed Mary Higgins, watching his arrival from her next door window . "You cooked my pet rabbit for dinner as I was sleepin' !"

"What, you watchin' for me ,missin' my cooking, MISS Mary Higgins ?"

Grandpa had brought me mosquito repellent and Vicks ointment to ward off the evil spirits that walked the grass at night. He had made a batch of Russian Cherries, .which were cherries aged for many months in a glass jar filled with sugar, some anise seeds and vodka.

-WIth the fervor of a lucky fisherman, out he pulled from the brown paper sack a special antique club he had lovingly polished for me, that which was historically known as a 'Rabbit Dunner'; for it mercifully knocked rabbits out of their consciousness. "Just like liquor, only quicker, " he would feverishly recite like an excited child coming home with a special prize.

He was one of the greatest hunters alive and had survived almost a hundred years on his many poached prizes. Grandpa claimed to be a Cree from Canada and part of the Maumee Tribe from Detroit. He worked the auto factory as a 'peacemaker' - breaking heads and knees.

But he didn't know what a bumper on a car was for, and he would tear the metal bumpers off his cars and strap on big Cedar Logs. Then he would put iron spikes through the logs. He did this to his Jeep Wagon and used it to chase through hills and valleys to 'spear' Buffalo.....He excused his creativity and told me that 'if one of us is going to live, it is going to be me !'..........

"Francy," Grandpa flirted. "Come over here. I have the pictures I took of you the last time I was here. Come look at how pretty you are !"

Tears ran down my face. "Grandpa, THERE IS NOTHING IN THE PICTURE ! IT IS BLACK ! WHERE AM I ? THAT IS NOT PRETTY ."

"Yes, it is VERY pretty," He cooed to me. "Your Grandma, her Sister, they always took the same picture. See, Francy, you could not capture their GRAVEN IMAGE, nor capture their souls, because they were always traveling far up above the earth, never still for a camera .....look..... up there in the white clouds.......now so fast........not even the White Winged Horses could catch up with them.......

෨෧

Proverbs 25- 2 : "It is the glory of God to conceal a thing: but the honour of kings is to search out a matter; The heaven for height, and the earth for depth, and the heart of kings is unsearchable."

෨෧

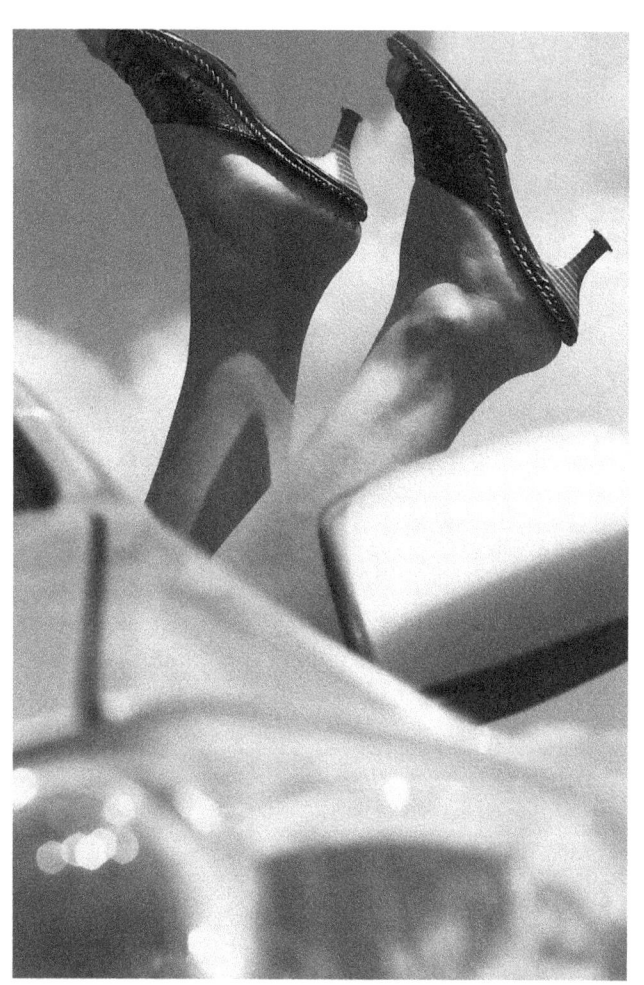

Going to San Antone'

Dr. Bannon's new Cadillac was not a Hearse because it didn't have any tassels swinging in the back, but it was looked almost like the car that my Dad sold to Mr. Binky, the owner of the town's "Gentleman's Club'.

Dad had added free shock absorbers for Mr. Binky to ride around 'really fat women' that he said a lot of men liked to see dancing around in their underwear. Mr. Binky would even lay the women down flat in the back of the Hearse and drive around town as advertisement for his club . Mr.
Binky did this because he said that men liked women who not only looked dead , but ones that also looked helpless and innocent……….

-But my Dad punched Binky on the nose when Binky told him that "Indian women had the fattest Nooky Twots of all, and that Mom could quit her ironing at any time." Mr. Binky paid him in full for the shocks.

"Wow, this Caddy is the ride of a lifetime !" Mizz Darla enthused.
"-Well, Kiddies - we are going to go see Doc's college roommate, Bob Reuter! He has built a special Museum called 'The Historic Cowboy Museum'. -And Bob says that you kids will never see anything this gory for the rest of your life !"

"No he said that for the money, you can't entertain the kids any cheaper or better," Dr Bannon whispered into Darla's ear……..

"Darla was doing the new women's liberation thing - which was driving and talking at the same time………….."Well, Francy, wouldn't you like to be one of Mr. Binky's Girls, or maybe be one of those cute Bond Girls in the James Bond Movie ?"

"No Ma'am, I want to be James Bond - because he does everything."

Dr. Bannon interrupted suddenly with a diverting cough. "You know, you would have to have the strength of James Bond just to wear on of those heavy, sequined costumes that Mr. Binky puts on those women !"

"Darla's eyes got real big. "So HOW would YOU know that, Doc ?"

"Dr. Bannon rationalized gently........Well, I see a lot of those women in my practice, honey. They have been abused"........

Thom clucked with a laugh "Yea, Mom, they all eat too much ! Mr Binky uses a funnel and a whip on them ! They look like Pigs, waddle like Ducks and eat like Horses !.....And Fart like Cows !""

"Shut up, Thom" warned The Doctor. "Yea, Bob said he did a really good wax diorama on the wars that escalated between the Karankawa Indians and the Texas settlers. According to Bob, the Karankawas did not do scalping - instead, they chopped off all the Texans' 'Whatchamacallits' and had weenie roasts ! Dr Bannon laughed and kept annoyingly pointing down to his lap.

As The Doctor talked, it appeared that he was trying to not only engage his wife in conversation, but to revive within her something that had been lost with time and marriage ; to fascinate her again ; to connect with her on a primal level ; to again excite her interest in him............

"Yes," Dr. Bannon laughed, "The Karankawa women were given the settlers' scrotums to eat and the men ate the cache of wangs, or penis, for they supposedly tasted just like chicken necks. That is where they got the old saying 'strangling the chicken.'

"Ding Dongs and Twinkies," piped in Thom. "Dad, Is it true that those Karanka- was were actually just a bunch o' Messkins ?" (Mexicans)

"Thom, that is not nice....-No, Bob thinks that they migrated from Russia or Denmark, giving them the archeological name 'The Viking Indians' - they are just not sure if they came in the back door of Alaska or through the front door at Brownsville, Texas."..........

Everyone was humming along with sobering attention, surprised at what we were learning from The Doc. "We know that they were here before the Pilgrims came to Plymouth Rock, and Bob said he found a funny thing when they did a dig in Massachusetts. They found a pit with petrified poop, and it had intact, undigested corn kernels in it."

"Well, here's these Indians growing all this corn and no one could digest it ?........No, it was the Karankawa that could not digest it !
.....So it is believed that this biological alteration in this particular Indian led to severate relations from the other, more settled Indians - 'Pueblo Indians '

as some might say - and thus the Karankawa wandered with anguish all over Canada, USA & Mexico to discover their own customs.

The Caddy was bobbing like a Dolphin over the Hill country as the Doc's historic tutorial lead to more laughs . "Bob said that the Karankawas admired the white man and the large amount of children they had - and eating 'those' body parts would give The Karankawas the physical powers to keep their civilization afloat - to give them the physical and symbolic ability to multiply at better numbers."

"He means their peckers !'" roared Darla, who was getting all happy talking about her favorite subjects - but not about Indians, per se. "We all know after it is all said and done, all a man has left is his pecker !"

"Easy, Darla Honey,". whistled The Doc, as his eyes became lovingly attached to his whirlwind-driving wife. "this is a rough example of an Indian people and their human desire to love and to be loved - to find their own culture, their own religion..... to find something they could believe in.....something that would be the key to their survival. Survival by brute force was not enough. Wandering migration provided no home for the soul. The fittest had to have a strong spirit to guide them !"

"Is it an example of instinctively wanting to follow in the footsteps of The Lord without ever having known about the Bible - or did they ?......This is what we have been grappling with in the art of Psychology for some time - Man's understanding of his actions amidst all of the dark dimensions of ancient life........At least enough understanding for us to give them a reason for what THEY DID - or to give them forgiveness" ...

I did not understand the silence that ensued; I wondered in awe of who these peoples could have been ; for it seemed that I was the only one in the car that had rooted within me a primal fascination for these mysteries, instinctively preparing its way for me to believe in its answers, accept its knowledge, know its final truths......

Is that what this trip to San Antonio was supposed to be about ? - or would be about ?......-And what was I preparing for ?......Of course, none of my questions concerned ME, I mused to myself. I was just imagining things from an overly active imagination ....

33

Thom broke the thoughtful silence with a murmur in my ear. "I heard that 'yer Dad broke Mr. Binky's nose and he can't smell anymore…….."

⁊

Micah 7-18 : "Who is a God unto thee, that pardoneth inequity, and passeth by the transgression of the remnant of his heritage ? He retaineth not his anger forever, beause he delighteth in mercy."

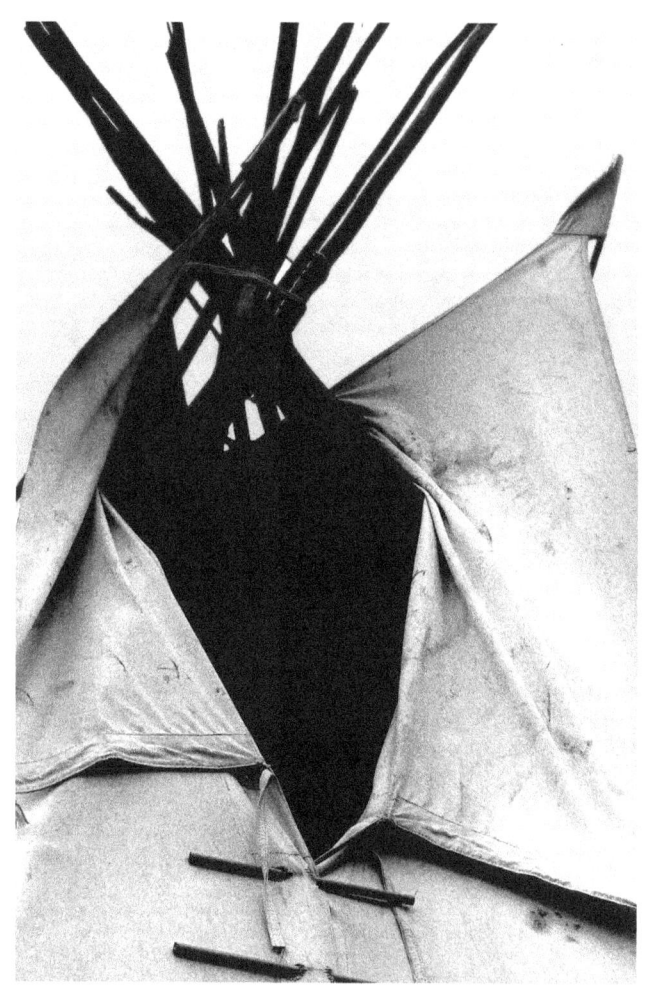

'THE ALAMO'

The Caddy became as quiet as a dropped stone in the middle of a hot asphalt parkway. We were here - a humid outcropping lined with dripping Desert Willow trees, their fine greenery being watered from the dew droplets wheezing out of the Caddy's Air Conditioning .

Hanging by a rustic chain was an intimidating sign in bold, ominous letters, an impression that flattened your breath on approach :

"The Famous Cowboy Historic Museum of San Antonio"
"This Museum Not For the Faint-Harted or Easily Farted"
"All Displays Historically Exact Replicas of the Times."

Upon entering the door, the cold wax of the museum met the warm outside air, bubbling a burst of falling mist around my body. I could not see, and little would I soon know that this would become an eminent omen, this familiar mist that I would see for the rest of my life; its signal to me that something was about to make itself known .

- A loud speaker was introducing a newly-formed line of eager visitors -

"As early as 1862, The U.S. Government drafted a mission to divert Civil War troops for annihilation of the Karankawa, but no General would carry out those diversion orders. So the Karankawas were loosely monitored from afar, sometimes by Union Submarines that surfaced into the Gulf Coast. Sometimes they were watched by Black 'itinerant soldiers', watchmen that knew the cotton fields & coastlines. "

"The original duty of the Subs was to keep the South from doing any trade or accepting any goods by sea, keeping the Southerners impoverished. The Union Army knew that they might have to wage war missions on The Karankawas if they allied with the Confederates . But they knew the consequences of they lost to them - mass castrations ! .... The U.S.
Government and the Union Army both felt that NO Indian could be trusted - that any Native American would take allegiance with whomever accrued the most benefits for them ."

The loudspeaker got even louder as we turned the corner. "But these sentiments were already being felt 50 years before in an already growing and culturally diverse Texas - Yes, Texas, folks - a state that was already ahead of its time ! Welcome everybody to the Historic Cowboy Museum !"

An Old, Grey Man appeared with a large cane. He was actually grey all over like he had been dipped in formaldehyde. It was Bob Reuter, Doc Bannon's old roommate. "Hello, everyone, I am the director of the museum, Bob Reuter. Today will be your day of REVELATION !"........

....."Yes folks," He blurted out with the style of a Circus Master.. "You are not going to like everything you hear today, but fable has a way of becoming truth - especially when there has been archeological research to either question an old fact or to back up a new one."

The revolving diorama revealed itself from behind an automatic curtain, and with it highlighting some of Mr. Reuter's more controversial introductions of Texas history ....

"The wife of Mexican General Santa Anna came up with a very strategic military concept for her husband," Mr. Reuter forcefully stated. "The Karankawas would be bribed and misled by the Mexicans into raiding the Alamo in exchange for eternal life that would be specially given to them by the Church. They were told that the white man they admired would be soon killing THEM, just like the Rabbit and Buffalo, in efforts to enrage the Karankawa with notions of betrayal. "

"We now know that it was The Karankawa Indians - NOT The Mexican Army - that waged attack on the Alamo ! They who became drunk with their angry hearts.....THIS is what lead to the grisly deaths of Jim Bowie, Davy Crockett and many other unaccounted numbers of those that bravely fought for an autonomous and free Texas Republic- a Texas free from Mexico."

Mr. Bob Reuter annotated the audience to the display of an old, frayed diary in one of the revolving dioramas, a diary supposedly from an anonymous servant who served and slaved with forgotten loyalties.....

"Such unfair connivery should not have had any place in this war. Mexico should have stepped up to the plate and fought this war themselves. By all standards, this was an unfair war, a war that the Texans did not have to lose ; and with hindsight and in foresight, it MUST be the Texans who should remind

Mexico to 'Remember The Alamo' the next time that Mexico wants something from the USA."

Mr. Reuter's voice then turned apologetic. "Let's just say that a caring Wife who did not want to lose her husband created a lot of historic and political atmospheres for Texas that probably never needed to be."

To everyone's awe and embarrassment, Thom's voice blurted out with a tortured, raging excitement. "It takes 100 Mexicans to get the lead out, but It takes only one mad Karankawa to gut out your belly ! Bowie and Crockett would have NEVER let themselves die from just a bunch of scrawny Mexicans throwing stale tortillas at them ! "

Doctor Bannon quickly took Thom aside where he proceeded to whip his son's butt into the raw, reddish-blue color of vine-ripened Uvalde Berries, warmed by dawn's light before the Javelina Hogs could descend on them.

Darla tried to woo me from her embarrassment, her head tilted toward me in a low voice, feigning intense interest. " Francy, I don't see any mention here of our gorgeous hunk, Sam Houston, The Father of Texas..."

-But then suddenly, Darla brought about everyone's attention by pointing to something with a frightened snap of her wrist, almost as if she was warning a flock of sheep to an impending
 Wolf stalking the horizon..........

"FRANCY, I didn't know YOU were a Karankawa !" exclaimed Darla.

...........and there it was for all to see and for me to realize..........

The new exhibit featured an imposing Karankawa man protecting woman and child while he was putting a Bowie knife into the belly of a bearded settler who had tried to shoot him with a musket gun.

...........and there it was for me to see and everyone to realize........

The Karankawa man in the diorama was, undoubtedly, as everyone could see, an unmistakable REPLICA of ME ; from the top of my head to the bottom of my feet ; the baby was identical to my baby pictures...

Everyone in the museum turned around to inspect my presence, distancing themselves away from me as though I suddenly had developed a bad smell.

"Oh, Jesus, Oh my God !" exclaimed Bob Reuter. "I thought they were all EXTINCT! Come here, little BOY ! Don't let him get away !"

Frightened into running out the door and hiding behind a tree, I wanted to get away from the pointing and staring, not knowing in my heart if I would be invited for a ride back home. It was a long way, home was.

- IT WAS THE DAY OF REVELATION WHEN I DISCOVERED THAT THE ALAMO WAS NOT THE WHITE HOUSE -

It was purely accidental that I had discovered who I really was; learning about something that I never before had any reason to learn about .

After all, my family - without any question, I thought - was from France.

The trip back home was long, silent and tedious.

No one spoke of the museum exhibit.

No one spoke to me.

Mrs. Bannon looked into the rear-view mirror with fear.

I sensed that no one wanted me in the car.

 The Bannons dropped me off in the driveway of my house without talking to my Mother.

I never saw any of them again. Never again.

Thom disappeared and went to live with his grandmother.

Dr. Bannon called my Father and said that I was fine and he could no longer do anything to help me.

-As more and more people in the neighborhood went on the weekends to see the museum, I clearly was not welcome to visit at anyone's house anymore, and the neighborhood became silent and barren.

Without the touch of communication, my life had become listless and unbearable, my invisible presence adrift beyond a remote void. ....

- A moment frought by mysterious accident had led to my discovery of God's-

.... SHAME...................

Its world of
        disgrace sown
A universe of
        distain grown
Not with mine
     own doing
But of the doing
     of those
          before me
Of a generation past
     now happening
               before mine seen
The Son of succession
     now languishing
               behind mine been

Of a time last
     Invisibly apparent
               to the Father I now see
The apparition
     For a generation
          as The Holy Ghost past in me

∽

Micah 7-1 : "Woe is me! For I as when they have gathered the summer fruits, as the grapeleanings of the vintage: there is no cluster to eat: my soul desired the first ripe fruit !"

The pickle cabinet

A good Marriage has the crisp scent of pickles, its robust cloud of vinegar stinging your nose; Its companionship languished like the heavy morning smell of sweet, dewy peonies rooted in musten earth. This was just one of the simple things I effortlessly enjoyed, but just one of the many valuable things learned in my early years of naïve womanhood :

That the white house was in Washington, DC, - not in San Antonio.
That Sam Houston was not the President.
-And that marriage, like canning, would quickly turn to sour poison if anything was lost in its process.

Near the back kitchen door was my wonderful Pickle Cabinet, more of a large closet than a cabinet; at 6 feet wide by 12 feet deep, with its pungent scent of pine and cedar shelves, its cold stillness of stainless and glass softened by sweet -agar .

Pickling in the Pickle Cabinet had become the sole reason I spent most of my time, secondary to hiding from my marriage to John.

One day I decided that I would never come out of the pickle cabinet.

I had readied a safety lock inside the cabinet door, and carved an invisible slit near belly-high into the door slats ; now I could see who was at my door. It was usually John.

"Where's my dinner, you stupid Dike Bitch ! Get your damn ugly Dike ass outa' there !"

"Honey," I asked, "Do you want some pickled Pigs' feet ? They go very well with your Ale and Chips I will be out in a minute…….. "

"Naw, I want your butt out of there NOW. What the shit did you do today, dirty old plumbing stuff ? You Lesbo, I should have dated Ann."

"Yes, Dear," I replied, "she had a nice, low Intelligent Quotient. They say that it is as good nowadays as having a low Cholesterol Count. Because now doctors can always inject some fat cells where they are needed or missing, or wanted, or whatever."

"You say to ME whatever? You are NOW a DEAD Dike !"

I bent over to look through the slats and John had MY gun shining into MY cabinet, ready to shoot open the lock. Obviously, he had finally had enough of me. I grabbed my butcher knife from behind the flour.

................."Come and get me then."................

How the days
    Are strong
And the nights
    Are long
When one
    Has something to say
And cannot say it
    How the
        Road so long
           And the heart forlong
When one
    has nothing to say
        And wants to say it

I picked up the phone and called Amarillo.

"Grandpa, I killed John. He got real mean again and he was going to kill me. Right now, MY gun is STUCK in HIS hand........

Grandpa seemed relieved, puzzled and excitedly entertained all at the same time.

"Francy, load him in the tub, and I will get a bus ticket. This same thing happened to your Grandmother's Sister when she was only 27 . But she was held hostage on a boat and the bastard fell overboard, like a big Carpfish. Well, not even the sharks would have him, and they found him preserved in algae.... Hey, Francy, remember when we went fishing ? ....Well, don't go anywhere, 'cause I will be there," as he poetically ended our call. Grandpa always liked to create rhymes and poems.

Cold circles of semantics ran through my blood; I was organizing a purpose for my actions, allocating my motivations to absolve my actions. I had discovered the calculating excuses, the disagreeable anticipation of Terror.....

The only lone comfort wrapped around me was in knowing that all the neighbors would be cheering when they found out that John was gone.

I could tell them that John left me for another woman, or for another life, or that he had left to be in a separate world from all of us.

If I told the neighbors that he went to Heaven, they would all just laugh in utter disbelief.......... Yes that is what I would do...........

~

Proverbs 25-11 : "A word fitly spoken is like apples of Gold in pictures of Silver"

Grandpa arrived at the door smelling like a dirty bus, but he could not take a shower. John was in there.

"Well, Francy, " he exclaimed , "let's look at the bastard !" as he rubbed his stomach in pleasure. "Yea a lot of Union and non-Union guys in this old gut over the years. I still have a Gold ring with the initials 'JH' engraved on it, who-ever that was. That old Rabbit Dunner always got me promoted. I could come out of nowhere and get 'em !"

"Francy, you must go to the other room, Hon," Grandpa diplomatically asked of me. "Because this guy is not dead ! I have to kill him."

I heard the sounds of air escaping ; and a groan of whose voice I could not tell. "Francy, no worry," Grandpa motioned, "his spinal cord is nicked through, brain-dead, paralyzed. There are some keys in his pocket, Francy. You must tell me what they are to."

"Well, 'Gra'pa, they are to the car, the house, the safe. I have never needed to go in the safe- I make my own money doing some plumbing."

"We need to go in there, Hon-" -as Grandpa sternly eyed my shaking hands. " I want to know what this bad dude has been up to. If it is anything like what happened to your Aunt, then it was some bad stuff."

A hiss. A clank. There was no money in the safe, just wads of paper.
"Yes, here IT is," Grandpa read out loud to me. "This pays him Ten-Thousand Dollars upon your accidental death. He wanted to make you dead, Francy.......
Why ? Who else could be involved ? - How did he have your gun ?........Answer me, Francy. "

He looked at me with sullen eyes. "You hope that when a baby is born, that he will never experience anything that he will want to forget. You always wish that when he is old and dying that he will remember only that of a good life."

The walls started to spin out of control and suffocate me. I did not remember blacking out .... nor did I remember going into a comma.......

∽

Deuronomy 19-15 : "One witness shall not rise up against a man for any iniquity, or for any sin, in any sin that he sinneth; at the mouth of two witness, or at the mouth of three witness, shall a matter be established"

∽

Loved and lost
    A grandfather had a Son
He lost to war

Lost and loved
    A grandmother had a daughter
        she lost to domestic violence

One from afar
        the other next door
One with valor
        one with shame

Neither knows the value
        of what was lost
        of what was the same
        of what was levied
        of what was ascertained

Except through the whispers wandering
        spending away their sorrow
                with impoverished tears of rumor

the presence

I woke up looking straight at a woman who I did not want to look like twenty years from now……….
"You are in the hospital, Honey, and your 'Pa Blue Fox is next to you. Can you see Mr. Blue Fox, your Grandfather, Hon ?"

The Nurse apologized with a tear. "You came in barely breathing, but they could not find anything wrong with you except that you were pregnant. You had an attack of the runs while you were passed out. We could not stop what was happening and you pooped the baby out dead. You've been out for over five days. We are so sorry, Honey."

"Yea, she tried to eat her husband and got sick.'" grinned Grandpa.

The Nurse heartily laughed. "Yea, I wish I could put my old man to use like that, as he sits in front of the TV all day while I am here in the hospital dealing with poo, pee & vomit."

"Do you deal with Semen?" Grandpa laughed , staring at her butt.
"You dirty Old Indian," The Nurse rebuffed. "As soon she pees on her own, you can call me to get discharged outta' here !"

Grandpa winked as the nurse snarled at him in disgust. His voice became gentle, focused soft upon my eyes, his eyes CLOSED……

"Let me LOOK at you Francy, lying here, just like your grandmother. She was in perfect health until one day she turned black and blue all over her body, like she was bruised, but she was not. They said she had malignant Diabetes, and she died three days later."

"We were so lucky when we had your Mother, as your Grandma almost pooped her out dead, too. It had something to do with a blood enzyme she was born with that they knew nothing about, still don't after all these years. But you are here with me here and now - that is good."

My voice had become weakened with anxiety. "Grandpa, I guess I was out for a very long time. I had the strangest dreams ……….

"There was Grandma sitting upon a white horse, looking down at me with contempt, her face so angry and hateful. Instead of her black hair, she had a bunch of red, white and blue feathers, like a parrot. The feathers were falling out of her scalp, falling to the ground and blowing into the wind . She had a face and neck like a Vulture ......

......She motioned quickly for me to get on the horse with her, but I was too scared to move. She then haughtily turned around and ran away with her horse's back to me, taunting me, daring me.......

Somehow, I got the feeling that she would be back for me someday ....Just the feeling of knowing that IS the nightmare of my dream."

As strength came over me, Grandpa helped me to the bathroom. He grabbed my wrist so hard, so urgent, so furiously ; it was as if he were desperate to get my attention for the very last time.

"Francy, they will be quick to condemn you. But I know that you were just protecting your baby. Did you know that you were pregnant ?"

Silence overshadowed the conversation as we left the bathroom . "Let me call the Nurse and ask her for a date," Grandpa mused. "But you must know that your Grandma was not angry at you in the dream. She now lives in a dimension where she sees the worst of man's transgressions as they are revealed to her, victims & perpetrators alike ....

She sees their past they vaguely forget
Their pain they want cured forever
Their hopes they cannot remember entirely
Their wants they still linger intently
Their wishes for retribution they desire infinitely

 "Remember, Francy, she is in a place where she can really do nothing but only know ; she is the vessel for their stories, for their confessions - as they are parting from this world. They ALL must pass through her presence to get permission to get into Purgatory, then MAYBE into Heaven. "

"They could get a second life that is free from the pain they felt, freedom from knowledge of their past actions, freedom from their guilt, blessed and absolved through their newly-born innocence."

" Francy, I believe - No, I KNOW - that your Grandmother was ordained by God to be the keeper of Purgatory, the Judge that hears all testimony without judgement. She told you by her presence that she wants you to be her apprentice. "

Deuronomy 4-9 : "Only take heed to thyself and keep thy soul diligently, lest thou forget the things which thine eyes have seen and lest they depart from they heart all the days of thy life, but teach them thy sons, and they sons' sons."

.... "Grandpa, I see that much of the nightmare in my dream is where Grandma's Horse is perched upon a muddy crossroads, trying to turn around on a slippery slope; it is there I can become a very good person or a very bad person, nothing in between. I know that after what has happened to me that I can never go back to the same person that I was ever again; and I am on a lost, untreaded path."

∽

Jeremiah 24-3 : "Then said the Lord unto me, What seest thou, Jeremiah? And I said, Figs; the good figs, very good; and the evil, very evil, that cannot be eaten, they are so evil."

"Thus," saith the Lord, "Like these good figs, so will I acknowledge them that are carried away captive of Judah, whom I have sent out of this place into the land of the Chal-de'ans for their good; and I will plant them and not pluck them up; and I will give them an heart to know me; and they shall be my people, and I will be their God; for they shall return unto me with their whole heart."

The Nurse interrupted our conversation with a lighter mood, needing our discharge signatures. "Looks like Blue Fox forgot to bring you some street clothes, so we won't charge you for the gown - I don't think your Grandpa wants you to leave naked , do you, Blue Fox ?!"

Grandpa shamefully avoided eye contact, further escalating the flirting. "Yea, I could not get the car started, either, so we have to wait on the street for the bus."

"Oh, you are so cute - really charming" the Nurse admitted with tired admonition, looking
down at Grandpa's child-like manner...

                                        ᑲ

I Corinthians 12-4 : "Now there are diversities of gifts, but the same spirit. For to one is given by the Spirit the word of wisdom; to another word of knowledge; to another, faith; to another the gifts of healing ; for as the body is one and hath many members of that one body, being many, are one body: SO ALSO IS CHRIST."

THE LAST VISITATION

"Guess she liked my talents," Grandpa whispered as we waited on the warmed Transit bench "Her name & phone number is on the bill ! I'm going to call her and ask her why there is a charge for a semen container."

Laughter turned into dire seriousness, he grabbing me with reddened face , my neck crouched down to my knees in his angry , hard palm.

"Never, NEVER get on that horse with your grandma. She will come to you one lonely night, begging you get on for a joyride into the dusk, to chase those glorious colors of sunset. Then you REALLY will never be the same again. And your hair will turn into falling feathers !"

"OUCH, Stop !" I begged ; His grip only got harder, my neck burning under his thumb as he violently disciplined me in front of stalled traffic.

"Francy, the RED feather is for bloodshed, retribution for your trespass; The BLUE feather is our regret and sorrow for what must be done, what will be done; The White feather is for our contrition, believing we can relinquish with repentance, believing we can foolishly and vainly ask for forgiveness and Salvation."

"But there is NO absolution, NO resurrection for us ! We are NOT Christ , and we can NEVER be !" he seethed through his teeth.

"Francy, I specifically asked you if you knew you were pregnant or not, as this aspect could be very important in the eyes of the Law - but I get no answer from you. What am I supposed to think ?"

ᗆᕲ

Galatians 2-16 : 'Knowing that a man is not justified by the works of the law, but by the faith of Jesus Christ, even we have believed in Christ, that we might be justified by the faith of Christ, and not by the works of the law: for by the works of the law shall no flesh be justified.'

"Listen to me, Francy, you have to absorb John's spirit or his spirit will come back to get you . You have to show God that John did not die in vain. No being shall ever die in vain, whether he be man or beast, that is our foremost Universal belief."

"So you think Jesus rose from the dead just because he could? Francy, you better not be a liar to me. I see a lie in your silence. Was it all an accident? Are you fooling me? I will make you eat what you have killed. I will make sure that you will not be a spoiler in my eyes."

I was relieved when the Bus arrived, not a moment not too soon. Grandpa let his grip go of my neck and poetically laughed at me like a madman. "You will eat his soul-so he can go-go down the commode."

∾

Ezekiel 3-17 to 3-19 : 'Son of man, I have made thee a watchman unto the house of Israel; when thou not speakest to warn the wicked from his wicked way, to save his life; the same wicked man shall die in his iniquity; but his blood will I require at thine hand......

......Yet if thou DO warn the wicked, and he turn not from his ways, he shall still die in his iniquity; -but thou hast delivered thy soul.'

∾

The bus delivered us back to my home, its silent air breathing through its walls ; its breathless notice waifting through its unfulfilled space, watching our every emotion.......

It was as though John had never existed. But It was not such a big thing after all, much as I had told myself many years ago ; he was now in the freezer, wrapped in little parcels of white butcher paper............

"I was busy while you were in the hospital for all those days." lovingly smiled Grandpa Blue Fox. "Lets go look in the cabinet - I have the skill of an artist, that of a generation of artists of which no one ever sees."

For I would say to myself that he was more than just an artist in his eyes ; I wished with the eyes of a child that he belonged only to me, forever with me.......Was he now delivering to me his gift of forgiveness ?

"I want to tell you, Francy, that you grew up to be a wonderful woman. I know you will always do right by me, do right by God. I know that I will never have any bad dreams about you, never. That is all I ever want to know."

Grandpa reached up onto the shelf, straining from its height, when out from hiding paraded a pickled penis, complete with onions and pimentos, beautifully sealed in a crystal jar. It looked not much different than the adored delicacy of the pickled Pig's Feet bought at the Deli..

"Man, that bastard's 'foreskin was tough - Well, Fancy Francy, I pickled his Pickle," Grandpa laughed, as he quoted another one of his adult nursery rhymes.

......But THAT little delicacy I would leave for Grandpa, when he comes back to visit me; but who I knew would never be coming back to see me.

Somehow we both knew this, but I would tirelessly tease him about it one more time, testing both fate and future; for the migration of the Karankawa is but just endless wandering, a forlong wanting that is not there.......

.........for something that will be nowhere to be found..........

"Stay with me for the rest of my life, your life," I asked of him........

"We would just get tired of each other after awhile," he would say to me.

But he did visit   A dream one lone night
                            Said he came from over the hills
                            From a place in India so he said
Over There   Where the horses now roam
Over Here   Where the mice drink sacred milk

For He   To set my soul at peace
For never to be   No war
But no never   Should my soul be at peace
                            A peace from which I awoke
And it was   Just a little spider
                                 crawling up the wall
               When he looked back at me
                           with eyes of discovery
And it told me   All will be done
                                 man can reach the Sun
               When Horses Fly

A Sermon For Our New Decade

-Today RECEIVES the year 2012, and a century REALIZED since my Grand-parents married each other away from their reservation in Quebec.

-But back then, 'Injuns' were not supposed to uppity and go - but to idly wait by to RECEIVE what would be discarded or abandoned - to then later REALIZE the aftermath of what would be reaped and gleaned.

-And so we must always be vigil of the fact that these two words, as they both exist together - to RECEIVE and to REALIZE - will become our most important gateway towards our spiritual discoveries.

-Through the graces of God, these two words will never be apart, as they actively work together, in inherited unison, hand in glove, as life unto death, from seed to harvest...........

-That of Receiving becomes our prelude to giving, to accept and to make welcome God's gifts that are here for us to discover.

-That of Realizing becomes our prelude to discovery, to recognize and understand God's effort to make perfect - to realize THAT which is not imminently present - but surely IS here........

-And as we keep vigil unto the aftermath of our actions, unto the forethought of our blessings, we will see that these words will always come together to speak unto themselves, to speak unto our actions, to speak unto us :   For they will tell us that to receive and to realize is to be accepted into-and to be made perfect through-our entering the Kingdom of God.....

Galatians 3-26 : "For ye all are the children of God by faith in Christ Jesus."

61

DISCOVER MORE OF
THE KARANKAWA OF TERLINGUA

COMING SOON.............

"VISITATIONS FROM THE SCHOOLYARD"

..........can the powerless innocence of an unsuspecting child thwart the devices of the powerful?

www.ingramcontent.com/pod-product-compliance
Lightning Source LLC
Chambersburg PA
CBHW071209130626
46555CB00004B/1636